AF228588

THE WORLD'S FASTEST BOATS

A&D Xtreme
BOLD HI-LO NONFICTION
An imprint of Abdo Publishing
abdobooks.com

S.L. HAMILTON

TAKE IT TO THE XTREME!

GET READY FOR AN XTREME ADVENTURE!
THE PAGES OF THIS BOOK WILL TAKE YOU INTO THE THRILLING
WORLD OF THE FASTEST BOATS ON EARTH.
WHEN YOU HAVE FINISHED READING THIS BOOK, TAKE THE
XTREME CHALLENGE ON PAGE 45 ABOUT WHAT YOU'VE LEARNED!

ABDOBOOKS.COM

Published by Abdo Publishing, a division of ABDO, PO Box 398166, Minneapolis, Minnesota 55439. Copyright © 2021 by Abdo Consulting Group, Inc. International copyrights reserved in all countries. No part of this book may be reproduced in any form without written permission from the publisher. A&D Xtreme™ is a trademark and logo of Abdo Publishing.

Printed in the United States of America, North Mankato, MN.

032020

092020

THIS BOOK CONTAINS
RECYCLED MATERIALS

Editor: John Hamilton; Copy Editor: Bridget O'Brien

Graphic Design: Sue Hamilton; Imprint Template Design: Dorothy Toth

Cover Design: Victoria Bates

Cover Photo: Alamy

Interior Photos & Illustrations: Alamy-pg 41 (bottom); Allison Boats-pgs 4-5 & 30-31; David Dilks-pgs 28-29; Cigarette Racing Team/Mercedes-AMG-pgs 32-33; Jaguar-pgs 24-25; Jimmy Biro/SpeedontheWater-pgs 36-37; Library of Congress-pgs 6-7; Midnight Express-pgs 26-27; Miss Geico Racing Team-pgs 34-35; MIT-pg 13; Mulder Design-pgs 22-23; National Archives of Australia-pgs 42-43; Red Line Synthetic Oil Corp-pgs 38-39; Shutterstock-pgs 8-9 & 10-11; Steve Finberg-pg 12; The Bluebird Project-pg 40 & 41 (top); US Coast Guard-pgs 16-17; US Navy-pgs 14-15 & 18-19; Vestas-pgs 20-21; Warby Motorsports-pg 1 & 44.

LIBRARY OF CONGRESS CONTROL NUMBER: 2019956100

PUBLISHER'S CATALOGING-IN-PUBLICATION DATA

Names: Hamilton, S.L., author.

Title: The world's fastest boats / by S.L. Hamilton

Description: Minneapolis, Minnesota : Abdo Publishing, 2021 | Series: Xtreme speed | Includes online resources and index

Identifiers: ISBN 9781532193903 (lib. bdg.) | ISBN 9781098212681 (ebook)

Subjects: LCSH: Speed--Juvenile literature. | Motorboats--Speed--Juvenile literature. | Motor vehicles—Juvenile literature. | Transportation--Juvenile literature.

Classification: DDC 629.046--dc23

TABLE OF CONTENTS

CHAPTER 1

THE WORLD'S FASTEST BOATS

The fastest boats in the world use the most powerful engines combined with the most **aerodynamic** shapes to move across waterways in colorful blurs of speed.

Speed on water is thrilling, but dangerous. Racers have been killed when a boat hits a wave or object in the water. But the excitement of a new speed record keeps racers and fans coming back for more.

HISTORY

Thousands of years ago, Chinese dragon boats, Egyptian reed boats, and early canoes were some of the first vessels to race across rivers, lakes, and seas.

Dragon boat races in China.

Boats were powered by sails and steam in the early 1800s. Coal and **diesel** took over in the 1900s. Boat builders of the twentieth century used strong, lightweight materials. Jet engines brought the fastest boats into the future.

CHAPTER 3

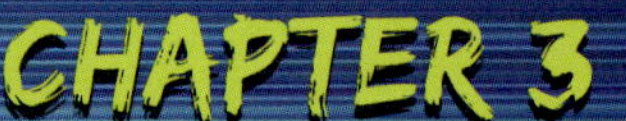

PILOTING & SAFETY

Piloting a boat requires knowledge of the area and its waters. This includes knowing underwater hazards, winds, tides, and weather.

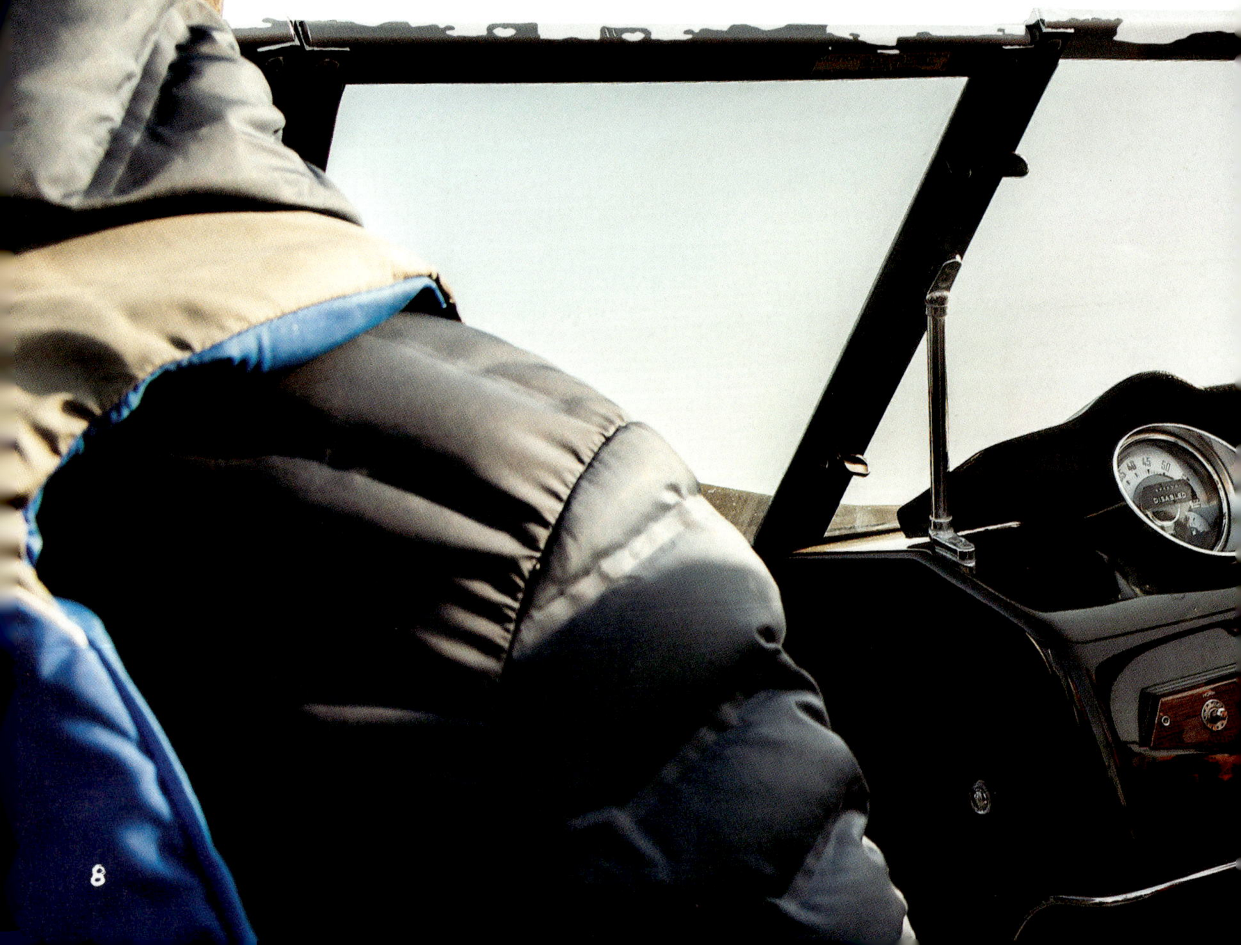

In general, a person must be at least 12-14 years old to pilot a boat. Many places require a person to complete a safety course and become certified.

A student trains to pilot a boat.

People who race fast boats wear helmets, goggles, and life jackets. Many life jackets have a small parachute in back. When it opens, a person's body hits the water with less force. Some racers wear **Kevlar** suits to protect their bodies.

Boat racers wear protective gear during a competition.

CHAPTER 4

SPEED BEASTS

The fastest human-powered boat is the Decavitator. Mark Drela brought the hydrofoil to a speed record of 21 mph (34 kph) on October 27, 1991. The pedal-driven boat was created by engineers at the Massachusetts Institute of Technology (MIT) in Boston, Massachusetts.

SPEED BEAST
CHARACTERISTICS

TOP SPEED RANGE
21-68 mph
(34-110 kph)

SPEED BEAST TYPES
Human-Powered,
US Navy Boat, US Coast
Guard Boat, Naval
Attack Boat

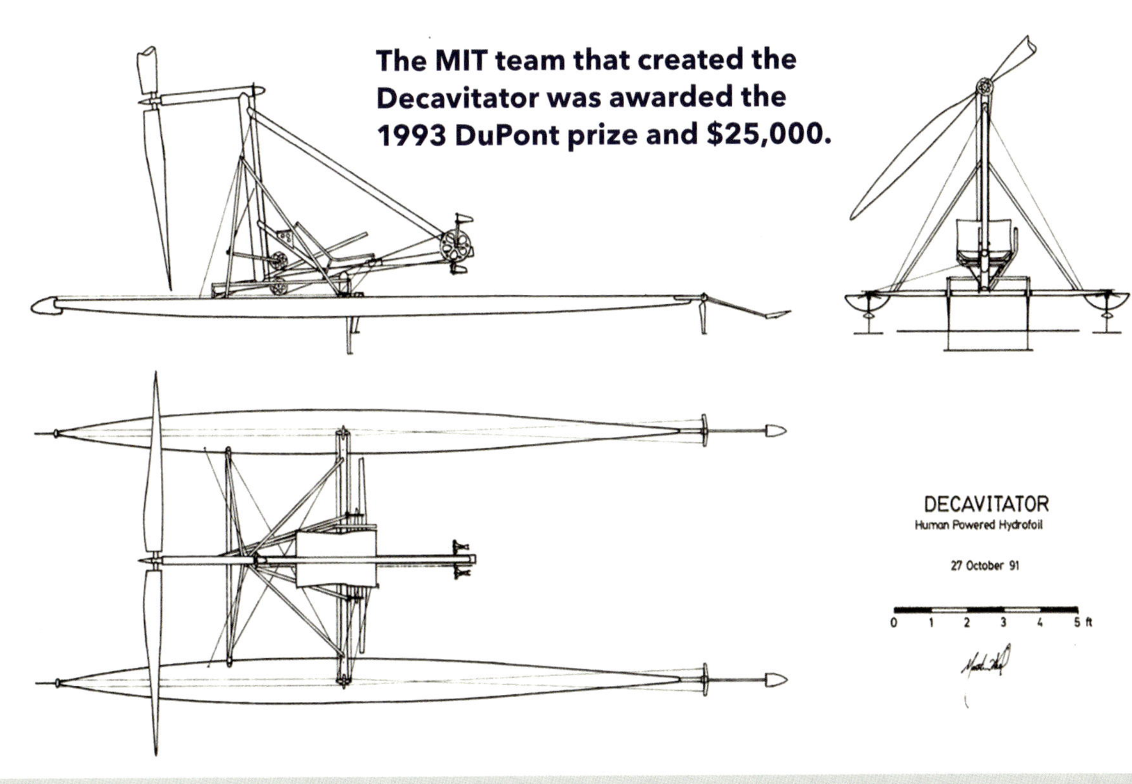

The MIT team that created the
Decavitator was awarded the
1993 DuPont prize and $25,000.

DECAVITATOR
Human Powered Hydrofoil

27 October 91

0   1   2   3   4   5 ft

The USS *Tucumcari* was the fastest US Navy boat. The special **prototype** hydrofoil gunboat reached a top speed of 58 mph (93 kph). The hydrofoils lifted the **hull** above the water. This allowed the ship to race across the surface, even in bad weather and heavy waves.

Tucumcari had a hydrofoil in the front, and one on either side of the boat.

Tucumcari launched
in 1967. The hydrofoil
performed successfully for
several years. It struck a
reef at night in 1972.

The US Coast Guard's fastest boat is a Defender-class special purpose craft. The 33-foot (10-m) boat has a top speed of 60 mph (97 kph). It helps Coasties catch **smugglers**, as well as reach shipwreck survivors quickly.

XTREME FACT

Defender boats are equipped with machine guns to protect and secure America's harbors.

The fastest naval attack boat is Norway's Skjold-class corvettes. These well-armed boats use waterjets to reach a top speed of 68 mph (110 kph). They can go from **idle** to full speed in less than a minute.

The Skjold-class corvettes are able to
turn easily even in shallow water or
at high speed.

CHAPTER 5

SPEED MONSTERS

The Vestas Sailrocket 2 has the record for the fastest **Class B sailing boat** in the world. Pilot Paul Larsen used only the sail to reach a speed of 75 mph (121 kph) on November 24, 2012.

The Vestas Sailrocket 2 was
built to beat the world record
and did so three times in a week.

The fastest super yacht is a Millennium 140 named *The World is Not Enough*. The 3-decked ship reaches a top speed of 80 mph (129 kph). Most super yachts travel about 29 mph (46 kph).

XTREME FACT

The ship can hold 15,000 gallons (56,781 liters) of fuel. With a full tank, it can go about 4,373 miles (7,038 km). That's like sailing across the Atlantic Ocean from Florida to Ireland!

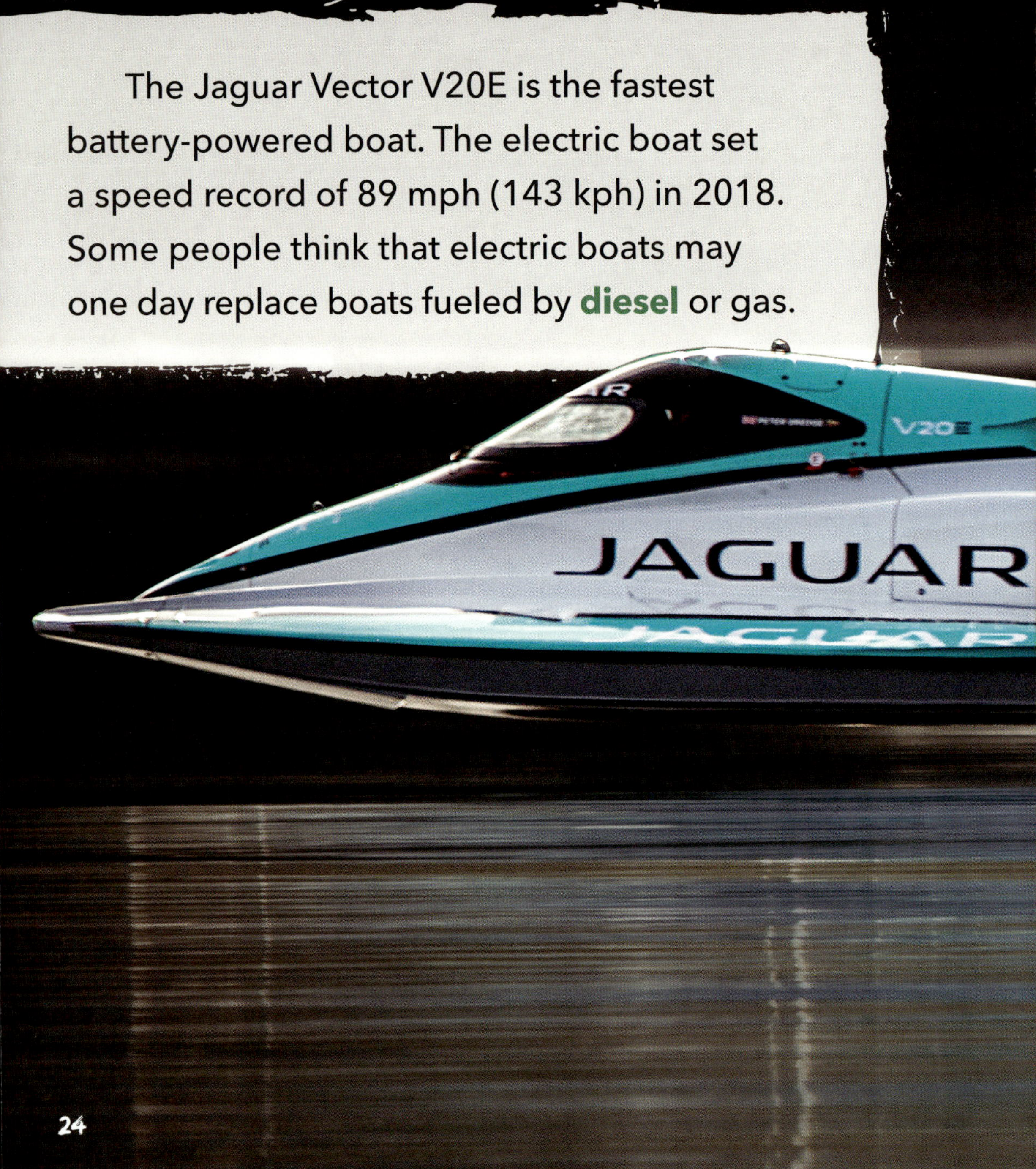

The Jaguar Vector V20E is the fastest battery-powered boat. The electric boat set a speed record of 89 mph (143 kph) in 2018. Some people think that electric boats may one day replace boats fueled by **diesel** or gas.

Before the Jaguar Vector V20E's 2018 record, the previous electric boat speed record was 77 mph (124 kph), set in 2008.

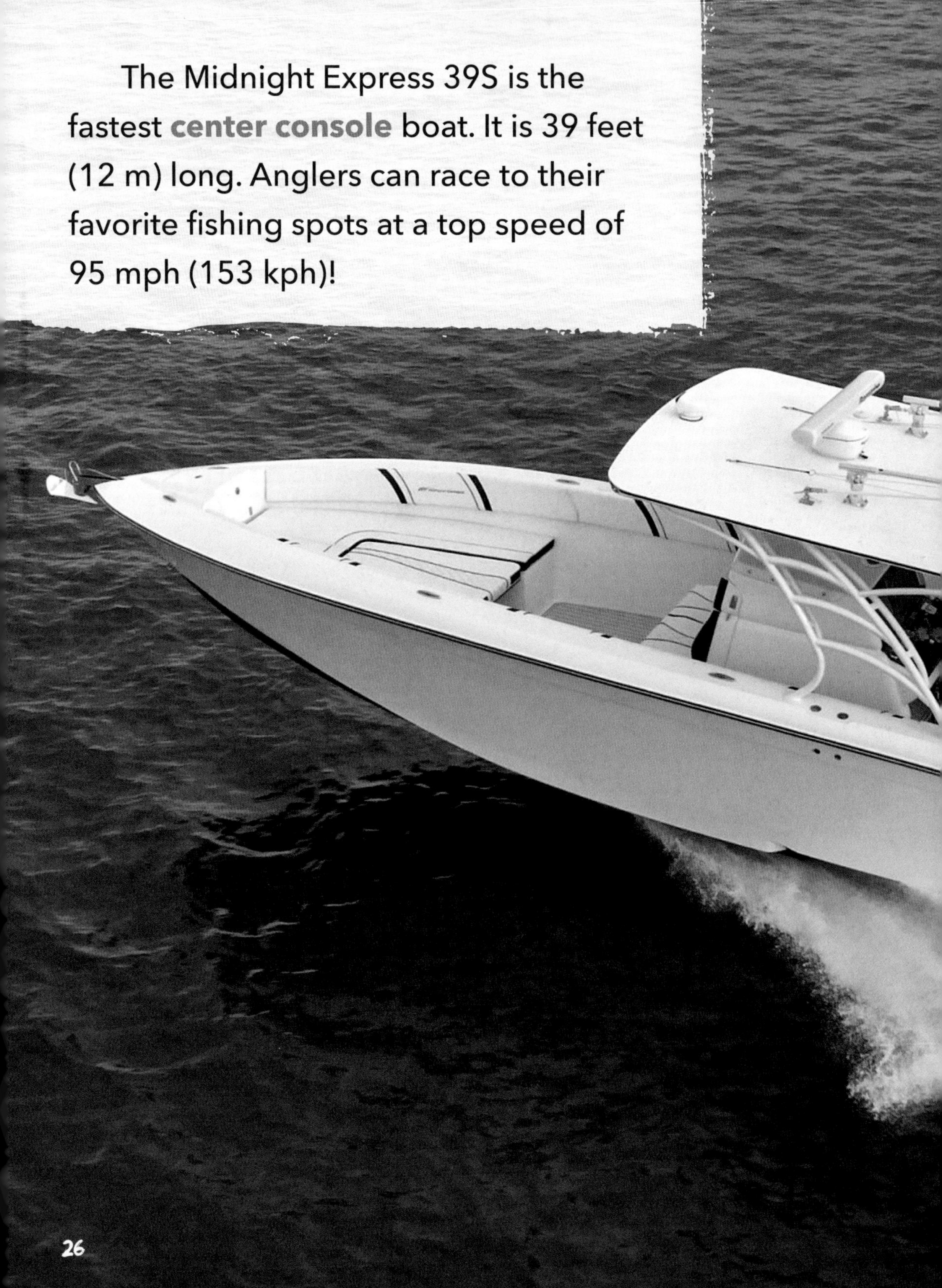

The Midnight Express 39S is the fastest **center console** boat. It is 39 feet (12 m) long. Anglers can race to their favorite fishing spots at a top speed of 95 mph (153 kph)!

The Midnight Express 39S reaches its top speed by using four powerful outboard motors.

CHAPTER 6

SPEED DEMONS

Many people think of a pontoon boat as slow, but a South Bay 925CR driven by Brad Rowland hit a speed record of 114 mph (183 kph). The 25-foot (8-m) -long pontoon boat named *Tooned In Two* was powered by three outboard engines.

SPEED DEMON CHARACTERISTICS

TOP SPEED RANGE
114-135 mph
(183-217 kph)

SPEED DEMON TYPES
Pontoon Boat, Bass
Boat, Go-Fast Boat

Brad Rowland someday hopes
to reach 120 mph (193 kph) in
his South Bay 925CR.

Bass boats are designed for freshwater fishing. To race across large bodies of water, especially during fishing contests, the top-speed Allison XB-2002 reaches 116 mph (187 kph).

XTREME FACT

Bass boats are known for their steadiness. Anglers can stand and cast even in rough water.

A go-fast boat is a craft designed for speed. It is long and narrow, and often equipped with multiple engines. The 50-foot (15-m) AMG Marauder GT S can race across the water at a top speed of 135 mph (217 kph).

XTREME FACT

Go-fast boats are also known as
rum-runners or cigarette boats.
Because of their speed, they are
sometimes used by smugglers.

SPEED FREAKS

Miss GEICO holds many offshore powerboat speed records. Racing driver James Sheppard and **throttleman** Steve Curtis have brought the *Miss GEICO* to a top speed of 210 mph (338 kph).

SPEED FREAK CHARACTERISTICS

TOP SPEED RANGE
210-318 mph
(338-512 kph)

SPEED FREAK TYPES
Offshore Powerboat, Catamaran, Top Fuel, Jet-Fueled Hydroplane, Custom Speed Boat

Miss GEICO won 10 World Championships and more than 100 individual races from 2005-2019.

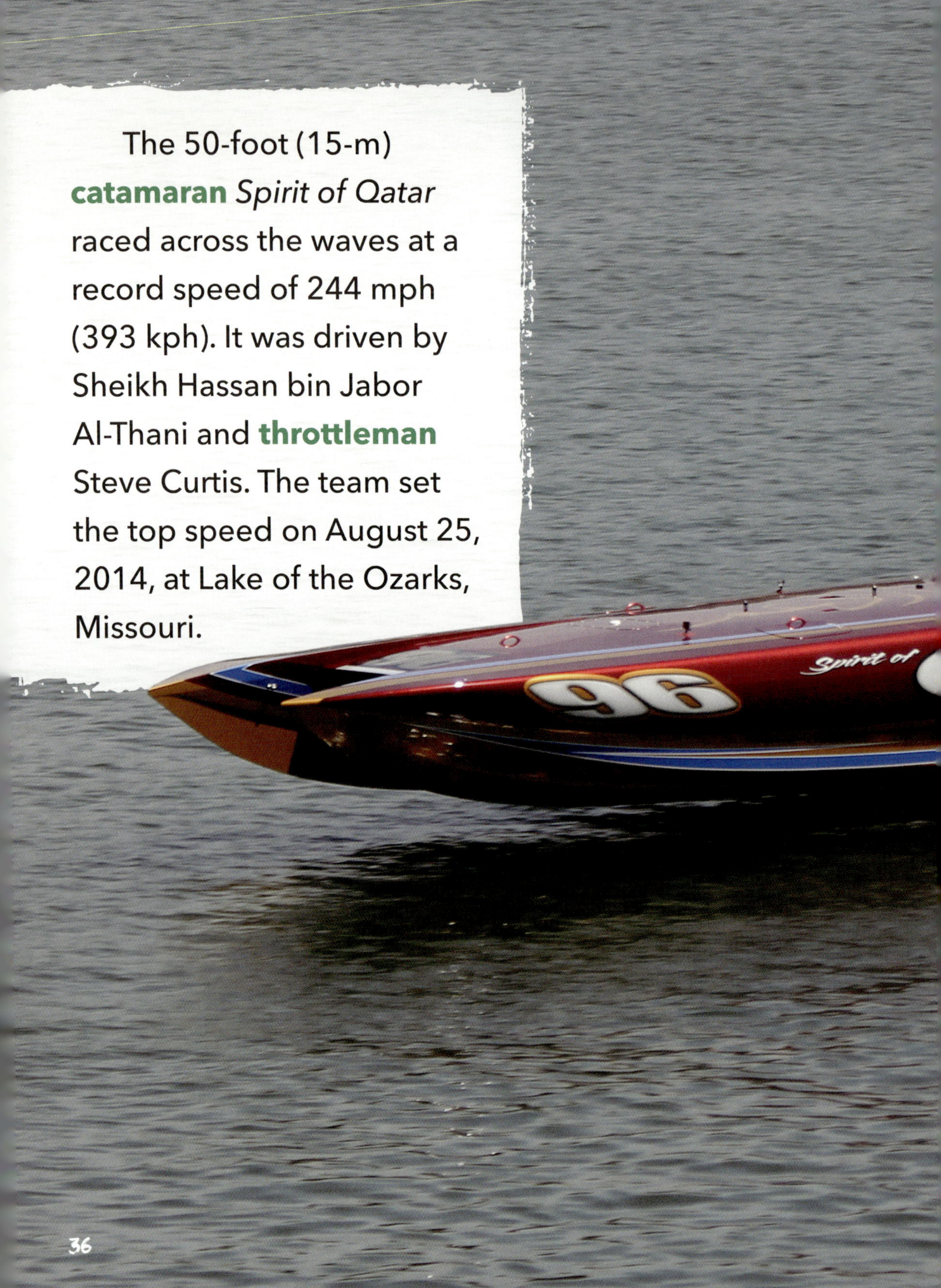

The 50-foot (15-m) **catamaran** *Spirit of Qatar* raced across the waves at a record speed of 244 mph (393 kph). It was driven by Sheikh Hassan bin Jabor Al-Thani and **throttleman** Steve Curtis. The team set the top speed on August 25, 2014, at Lake of the Ozarks, Missouri.

XTREME FACT

Spirit of Qatar was fitted with two 3,000-horsepower T-55 turbine engines to power it through the water.

The top fuel **hydroplane** *Problem Child* set a world speed record for a propeller-driven watercraft. Daryl "Madd Maxx" Ehrlich piloted the **drag boat** to a top speed of 262 mph (422 kph).

XTREME FACT

Problem Child hit its record speed in just 3.5 seconds. The top fuel hydroplane goes faster than a Formula 1 race car at its top speed.

Bluebird K7

Pilot Donald Campbell in his Bluebird K7 first took
the world's water speed record (WSR) in November 1955.
He reached 216 mph (348 kph) on Lake Mead, Nevada.
Campbell thought he could go faster. He worked on
the jet-powered **hydroplane**. On December 31, 1964,
Campbell took the K7 to an official top speed record of
276 mph (444 kph) on Lake Dumbleyung in Australia.

Bluebird K7 was brought up from its watery grave in 2001. It was rebuilt and may race again.

The fastest boat ever built is *Spirit of Australia*. It was created by Ken Warby of Australia. He bought an ex-military Westinghouse J34 jet engine for $69 and built a fiberglass and wood frame around it.

Ken Warby makes his world water speed record in 1978.

On October 8, 1978, Warby hit a water speed of 318 mph (512 kph) at Australia's Blowering Dam on the Tumut River. *Spirit of Australia's* record has yet to be broken.

XTREME FACT

Ken Warby is the only person to go more than 300 mph (483 kph) on the water and survive.

CHAPTER 8

FUTURE CONCEPTS

A new water speed record may someday be set by a fearless pilot using a powerful engine in an **aerodynamic** boat. Many pilots have died trying to beat Ken Warby's 1978 WSR, but new technology keeps people trying.

XTREME FACT

Ken Warby hopes his son will have the next WSR. David Warby has a jet fighter engine in his *Spirit of Australia II*.

XTREME CHALLENGE

TAKE THE QUIZ BELOW AND PUT WHAT YOU'VE LEARNED TO THE TEST!

1) What is the difference between a boat and a ship?

2) What dangers do speeding boats have that speeding cars do not?

3) What safety gear is needed for speed boat racers?

4) How quickly can a Top Fuel hydroplane reach its highest speed?

5) What type of boat may be used to move illegal cargo across the water? Why?

6) What is a WSR?

7) What is the fastest speed a boat ever reached? Who was piloting the boat?

GLOSSARY

aerodynamic – A smooth, streamlined shape that reduces the drag, or resistance, of air moving across its surface. Boats with aerodynamic shapes go faster because they don't have to push as hard to get through the water.

catamaran – A boat with two front hulls of equal size that are side by side. Also called "a cat."

center console – An open hull boat where the helm, or controls, are placed in the middle of the vessel.

Class B sailing boat – A sailing craft with 150-235 square feet (14-22 square meters) of sail.

diesel – A type of fuel that powers the engines of some boats, cars, and trucks. Gasoline also fuels some of these vehicles. Which fuel to use depends on the type of engine installed.

drag boat – A boat used for drag racing on the water. Drag racers speed down straight courses of varying lengths. Each racer tries for the fastest time to win.

hydroplane – A boat that rides on a cushion of air near the water's surface. This allows the boat to go very fast.

hull – The watertight body of a boat or ship. It may be open at the top (like a rowboat) or fully or partly closed by a deck.

idle – When a boat or other vehicle's engine is turned on and running, but not moving the vehicle.

Kevlar – A light and very strong man-made fiber. It is used to make helmets, vests, and other protective gear for sports, military, and law enforcement personnel.

prototype – The first of its kind. A model of something from which others are built.

smuggler – A person who secretly brings illegal goods into a country.

throttleman – A person who works as half of a two-person team in offshore powerboat racing. The throttleman controls speed, while the driver steers the boat.

ONLINE RESOURCES

To learn more about the world's fastest boats, please visit abdobooklinks.com or scan this QR code. These links are routinely monitored and updated to provide the most current information available.

INDEX